HIDDEN
WINGS

www.mascotbooks.com

HIDDEN WINGS

Editing provided by Emily Froc-Tarutis and Anita Lock.

For more information, please contact:
Mascot Books
620 Herndon Parkway, Suite 320
Herndon, VA 20170
info@mascotbooks.com

Library of Congress Control Number: 2020909720

CPSIA Code: PRV0820A
ISBN-13: 978-1-64543-416-0

Printed in the United States

*To all of those who have struggled to fit in
and those who were able to remain true to themselves.*

*To my amazing niece Antonia.
May you have the strength and courage to overcome any
obstacles that come your way.*

HIDDEN WINGS

Written and illustrated by

Sara K. Larca

Prologue

ONCE UPON A TIME ... many moons ago ... when the planets were still young ... trillions of souls went to and from a place high above the galaxies. Young souls were taught the ways of existence, and older ones came back to recharge and begin a new journey. There were no names, genders, or verbal language as a soul surpassed all of that, but in order to tell this story, universal traits must be assigned.

Each soul glowed with its own unique color, as every shade imaginable existed. This was how they were identified. Some souls were a single color, while others were a mixture of many. Souls were born the lightest shade of their particular color or colors, and each time they returned from Earth, they became brighter and more detailed. That is also how you could tell a younger soul from an older, more experienced one. There was no caste, class, or hierarchy, only learning, teaching, and sharing.

Souls wandered freely since there were no physical structures; only areas. There was a resting area but no beds, as souls did not need to sleep. There were meeting areas, but no kitchens or food, as souls needed only the energy that surrounded them to be nourished. There was teaching, and play areas, and everything in-between. As majestic as this haven was, there were—as there are everywhere now—dark and secretive places. While there were no areas that were specifically hidden, there were places that were much less visible for the safety of the young souls.

It was in one of those areas that a particular soul's existence was changed forever.

This is the story of Rain—short for rainbow—since her coloring was a combination of blues, greens, purples, oranges, and yellows.

As was mentioned previously, all souls, including Rain, were neither male nor female. For the sake of storytelling, Rain will be identified as female.

Time was another thing that worked differently here than it did on Earth. There were no days, weeks, or minutes, just then and now.

1

Rain was a curious and avid student, soaking up everything she could from her teachers and peers. She spoke to anyone and everyone with whom she crossed paths, hoping it would help her make the perfect choice. Her favorite thing to do was to wander around the area where the forms were. Every creature on Earth was a type of hologram, which made it possible to study from every angle, insides and all. Because Earth was so new, there weren't even amoebas and bacteria; organisms needed to help develop a new planet. But Rain wasn't interested in any of those. In fact, she wasn't really interested in any of the creatures displayed in this area.

Some souls spoke about wanting to slither on the

ground like a snake with no limbs to get in the way or hold them back, while others wanted to take the form of a bear so that they could sleep half the year in a warm cave. There was even a soul who wanted to be a rat so he could eat scraps all day, something that was intriguing to souls who didn't need food. That wasn't enough for Rain, though, because she didn't think that one form alone could define her.

Once during class, she mentioned her concerns to her teacher and was met with a frown.

"Well, the time will come for you to choose, and that's what you'll have to do," the teacher responded.

"But how can I choose when I don't feel an attachment to a single form?"

"There will be plenty of time for you to choose again; once your time on Earth has come to an end, you will be able to choose something else. In that way, you can be all of them."

"But—"

"No more of these questions; there are no buts, only decisions to be made." And just like that, the conversation ended.

Rain wasn't satisfied with these answers, which confused and disappointed her. It was the first time she realized that even though this place was so free and honest, there were things hidden from them, which made her even more curious. Once again, she found herself wandering around the forms area, going further and further than she ever had before, passing the snails and the roaches, the eagles and lions, and the salamanders and sharks. Eventually, the number of forms started to dwindle. As the sky began to darken, she thought that she had come to an end, until she saw a soft light ahead of her.

There was no fear in the galaxies, no uneasiness or worry since there was nothing that could harm the souls in this peaceful place. Rain ventured forward without a second thought; new forms slowly came into view, ones she had heard whispered about but had never seen for herself. There was a huge blubbery creature who lived in the sea with a horn sticking out of its head; a bird that was pink with tiny wings that somehow balanced on super long, skinny legs; and a deer who bounced on bent legs with a pouch on its stomach to hold its young.

Intrigued by all of this, she continued into the darkness until she came upon a handful of forms she never knew existed that were barely visible in the dim light. There was another horse-like creature with a horn sticking out of its head; a huge lizard with wings that had fiery breath; and something that looked like a bear but walked on two feet and had a kind face. It was then that she stopped dead in her tracks. Rain found herself face-to-face with a powerful white horse, boasting huge beautiful wings. At that moment, she knew who she was meant to be. The form had chosen her almost immediately, and she was quickly surrounded by a sense of calm. Rain was full of excitement but unsure of why these forms were not presented with all the others or their existence even discussed.

"What are all of these?" she said out loud to herself.

"The mixed ... and the forgotten," a quiet reply emerged from within the shadows.

Rain spun around, looking for the location of the sound. She was full of questions.

"Who are you? WHERE are you?"

Slowly a very dull grey soul appeared. There was no color, no spark, or light left in it. Rain had never seen a soul like this before, and it filled her with even more curiosity.

"I have no name," the grey soul whispered. "Soon, I won't even exist."

"What? How can that be? Souls go on forever."

The grey soul remained silent.

Rain ignored this since her curiosity about the new forms was stronger than the soul's obvious hesitancy.

"Where am I? Why are these forms here? Why don't we know about them?"

"These are 'the mixed,'" the grey soul responded. "The forms that are two in one, creatures that existed but never caught on, ones they don't want you to choose."

"What? But why not?"

"Because they want your time on Earth to be as easy and happy as possible. That means living as one being with a herd or a gaggle or a family of the same kind. They want you to make the 'right' choice."

"But we're souls! If we don't like what we choose, we can come back and pick again!"

"Yes, but not until your time is up; if you come back before then ..." the grey soul said, trailing off, sounding weaker and weaker by the minute.

"If you come back before then, what?"

The grey soul remained silent once again.

"Tell me what happens, please!" Rain pleaded, begging the soul for an answer.

"RAIN!! What are you doing over here?" shouted the teacher from a distance.

Startled, the young soul spun around. "I'm talking to ..." She stopped abruptly, realizing that the soul had never answered her question or given a name. She turned around to ask again, but the grey soul vanished back into the darkness from which it had come.

Rain turned back towards the teacher.

"I guess it left. I swear there was a grey soul here, and it was telling me all about—"

"About what?" the teacher questioned sternly.

"About this place, about these forms, about what happens if you choose to come back before your time on Earth is over."

"And what did it say?"

"Well, that these are mixed souls, ones who didn't

succeed on Earth. And that ... well, it never finished telling me what happens."

There was a moment of silence before the teacher finally spoke.

"We need to get back to the others. I suspect your time to choose will be soon."

"There are supposed to be no secrets here, so why are these forms hidden? And why haven't we been told about them? What will happen if you come back early? Please, I need answers!" Rain pushed.

"Very well," the teacher sighed.

While she wanted to argue this point and veer away from the conversation, she knew that she couldn't. The honesty and freedom the young soul had spoken of were not only true but the core of their teachings. It was one thing to try and shield them from future hardships and past mistakes, but it didn't feel right to blatantly lie when asked directly.

"These are where the mixed souls are kept. Since every soul is allowed to choose any form, some have been adventurous and created their own, a combination of two or more creatures. Some have succeeded with their time on Earth, unscathed by living a solitary life or lucky enough to have had other souls choose the same form as them, allowing them to start a new species. Those are the creatures you have just passed; the flamingo, the narwhal, and the kangaroo. While they survive, they are still not popular choices, which is why they are located further away."

"But maybe if they weren't so hidden, they would be chosen more?" Rain questioned.

"There is a system here. The creatures that are chosen more frequently are displayed closest to the front to help ensure the success of their species."

"Sooooo, the popular ones get more popular, and the rest get left behind?" Rain pushed back.

The teacher considered her statement for a moment but then shrugged it off.

"I don't know about all of that. This is just how it's always been."

While Rain was not at all satisfied with this explanation, she decided to let it go for the time being and move forward with the conversation.

"What about these ones back here?"

"These are the forgotten," the teacher answered sadly. "The creatures that didn't make it, that weren't accepted or chosen and are no longer a part of Earth's future."

"Why didn't they make it?"

"Oh, young soul, there is much for you to learn. Let us just forget about them, we can go back and help you find your form in the ... brighter area."

"I have already chosen a form. Well, actually, it has chosen me."

The teacher frowned as she followed Rain's gaze over

to the white horse with wings.

"What is it called?" the young soul asked.

"This is a Pegasus," the teacher sighed. "It means 'winged horse.' "

"Well, this is the form I'm meant to take."

"Rain," the teacher said calmly, "there are so many other wonderful, established creatures that will fill your time on Earth with joy and happiness. Why not just choose one of them?"

"I already told you, it chose me," Rain replied stubbornly.

The teacher just shook her head. "Well, there is still some time for you to think about what we have discussed, which I highly suggest you do."

The two quietly made their way back through the darkness towards the light.

Sensing her teacher's disappointment but still needing answers, Rain tried to get her to explain further.

"I'm sure souls change their minds all the time, right? But we're souls that exist forever, and with all these other options, I don't see what the big deal is."

The teacher stopped moving and looked at Rain.

"It is true that we come and go, choosing the same forms if we're pleased with them or trying out new ones if we're not, but there are rules and consequences."

"Rules? Consequences? Why is this the first I'm hearing of this? What are they?"

At this point, the teacher resigned herself to tell Rain everything she wanted to know.

"Rain," the teacher began, "when you choose a form, you are committing to that form for your entire stay on Earth. It can be for a short while or a long one, but that decision is in the Creator's hands. Living on Earth in a form that you don't connect with can be very hard, almost torturous, which is why we try and show you ones that have large numbers on Earth already. They can help you adjust. They will be there to celebrate the good times and support you through the hard ones."

"Why do we need to be with our 'own' kind? Why can't any creature be there for us?"

"Unfortunately, since the Earth is so young and the population is just beginning, there is a sense of comfort with the familiar. It is not like it is here, where everyone is the same. Once you are in your chosen form, you will begin to see the differences. It is only natural to be with those who understand you and your form because they are the same."

"That seems silly," the young soul scoffed.

"Perhaps it is, and perhaps one day, it will not be like that, but for now, it is."

"Well, I have many friends up here. Surely, we'll see each other again when we get to Earth. I know they won't care what form I chose!"

"I'm sorry, but it doesn't work that way. When you

arrive on Earth, you will no longer know the other souls."

"What? I'll lose my memory?" Rain barked.

"No, no. You won't lose your memory; you'll still know who you are, where you came from, and where you're going, but once a soul takes on a form, its colors are no longer visible, making it almost impossible to recognize them."

"But why?"

"I'd always assumed that it was to give everyone a fresh start, but I honestly don't know. Perhaps there's no real reason at all. Just make sure you don't pick your form based on the friendships you've made up here."

"Well why can't it be changed? Can't the Creator do something?"

"The Creator is just that, a Creator. It does not have any influence on what happens once you leave here. There are many obstacles on Earth that make it a difficult place to survive, but there are wonderful things there as well. That is the beauty of it. Souls get to experience a place full of conflicting ideas and choices, which helps them to learn and grow so that when they return to Earth the next time, they are stronger and wiser; and that is crucial to the survival of the planets and their species."

Rain thought for a minute, letting the words sink in.

"What happens if you choose to come back before the Creator has decided it's your time?" she asked once more.

"Everything stops."

"How so?"

"If you choose to come back early, you are considered unstable and no longer fit to go back. You can no longer visit Earth or any other planet. You can no longer choose another form." The teacher paused briefly. "You will be trapped here and grow weaker and weaker until, finally, the last of your light burns out, and you are no longer."

"No longer what?"

"No longer anything. You no longer exist. You disappear into nothingness. Or, at least, that's what we are led to believe. Eventually, those souls fade out, like the one you were talking about and are never seen or heard from again."

The teacher waited for a response or another question, but none came from the young soul; she just stood there in silence, trying to make sense of what she had just learned. Finally, Rain spoke.

"Why don't you tell the souls? Why don't you warn them?" She felt a warmth building up inside of her, a feeling she had never felt before. It would be a feeling that she would experience again during her time on Earth: anger.

"To protect you, of course. Our fear is that the younger souls will not be able to understand the reality or consequences of coming back early, and they might consider it a good option. Older and more experienced souls know that doing this is a terrible mistake. There are many times that you will feel lost or lonely or sad, feelings you can't possibly understand yet could cloud your judgment. Sometimes in the heat of the moment, it might seem like going back and starting all over is a great choice, the only choice. But it never is. And the worst part is that once that decision is made, it can't be unmade. We do lose some now and then, but it's only the saddest souls that come back early, the lost ones."

Rain shook her head. She understood what the teacher was saying and believed her intentions were good, but it didn't seem right. All these secrets, all these choices they have but don't know about. She had so many more questions about the grey soul and the fairness of it all. Even though she acknowledged how frightening choosing a lesser-known creature would be, she couldn't help but still feel drawn to the Pegasus form.

"So, we can become whatever we want. We can choose to be one of the lost or forgotten ... or even create something new?"

"Yes," the teacher replied, worried that Rain wasn't registering what she was telling her. "We cannot hold you back or tell you no. It is your time on Earth and your decision. But I beg you, young soul, to choose a form that is safe, that is known."

"I've already told you. My form chose me."

"I worry for you, Rain, but it's my job to support your decision. All I ask is that you keep what we've discussed between us. You might not like the fact that some things here are not an open book, but it is a decision made long ago and one that works. Please respect that."

Rain was unsure of keeping this new information to herself, but eventually gave in and agreed.

The two finally reached the brightly-lit forms area and parted ways, the teacher watching Rain as she disappeared into the distance.

"I hope she makes it," the teacher thought to herself.

2

"WHAT CREATURE ARE YOU GOING to choose," said one soul to another.

"Oh well, I'm definitely going to be a bird, so I can soar high in the sky! What about you?"

The second soul, definitive in its choice, replied, "I'm going to be a turtle! Then I can bring my home with me everywhere I go!"

"Ha! You are both thinking too small! I'm going to be a lion!!" chimed in a third. "King of the jungle!"

It did not escape Rain that all of these souls were planning to choose some of the most popular forms. Even though she had considered those options and all the others that had been presented to her previously, she couldn't help thinking about all the dimly-lit forms she stumbled across. After her conversation with the teacher, she made a valiant effort to find a "normal" form that she could connect with as strongly as she had with the Pegasus, but nothing had come even close.

Rain was drawn to the sky and to Earth alike. She could no sooner fight her truth than she could deny it, and eagerly awaited her chance to vocalize it. After what felt like forever, the young soul reached the front of the line, and face-to-face with the Creator.

The Creator, who was dazzling and intimidating, remained silent as Rain approached. It sparkled as beams of light burst from it, tiny fireworks flying off into the distance. The Creator knew that it was in the presence of a special soul, and these were moments it cherished.

"Hello, beautiful soul," the Creator said, finally breaking the silence. "Now, tell me, which figure would you like to embody for your time on Earth? I trust that you have thought long and hard about this and have chosen wisely."

"Yes, yes, I have," said Rain. "I'd like to be a Pegasus, please."

"Oh," replied the Creator. "Well, that's a very unusual request. I haven't heard one like that in many moons. Can you tell me how you came to this decision?" The Creator acted surprised, although it wasn't at all. The Creator expected something like this from a soul made up of so many brilliant colors.

"Well," Rain began, " I feel connected to the Earth and the sky equally. I didn't know how I'd ever be able to pick the right one until I found this form made up of both. It chose me; there was no decision to be made."

The Creator thought about this for a moment, carefully choosing its next words.

"Young soul, as you can imagine, I have been doing this for quite a long time now, and I've found that if you choose a mix of different creatures, you might find your life a bit more lonely and bit more difficult than most."

"Yes, yes," the young soul responded. "I have already spoken with my teacher about this and was warned about all the things that I might face by being different."

"That may very well be, but I must caution you once again. I've seen it all. I have been here since the beginning of everything. Unfortunately, I know what unhappy fate may await you down there. Many of the other souls might not understand your new form. While you are a young and unique soul with new ideas and information, many of the older souls that have been on Earth for a while are not accustomed to such differences. They stick to tradition, routine, and fear the unfamiliar."

"Oh ... well, I don't care about that!" Rain shot back quickly, "I will be so happy running and flying and exploring my new home that I won't have time to notice! Besides, things change all the time; I'm sure that there was a time when every form was new and young and went through hardships, yet so many have flourished. I'm sure it will all work out just fine," the soul added naïvely.

The Creator's head shook back and forth slowly, wondering what to do, considering that this soul's request could go terribly wrong and cause her world to be full of confusion and pain. Yet, it had faith that her uniqueness and confidence would help her prevail.

"Alright," the Creator finally responded. "I will grant your request, but you must promise me that you will remember our conversation and remain true to yourself, no matter what happens. While you're on Earth, this will be your permanent form, so you'll have to live with it either way."

Rain paused for a split second, remembering the story of the lost souls, and a pang of fear ran through her, but she pushed it away. She was strong and confident, unwilling to believe that her time on Earth could ever be so bad that she would even consider coming back early. If anything, the warnings had become nothing more than a challenge for her.

"Of course, and I promise," she finally answered. "I'm not worried about it. It's going to be great! Who knows? Maybe others will follow my path, and we will bring that form back to popularity."

Rain had made up her mind. She was unwilling to budge on her decision. Since there was nothing left for the Creator to do, it turned her into a beautiful white horse with a long, flowing mane and strong feathered wings.

"Now, all that's left to do is choose your Earth name—"

"How about Horid for horse bird! Or even Pegasus, as that's what I'll be!" the young soul interjected excitedly.

This made the Creator chuckle. "No, beautiful soul, you cannot be named after your 'own' species. If others do follow you, it will surely get confusing. I think we should call you Rain. It is a tribute to your brilliant rainbow coloring, and perhaps it will serve as a reminder of who you really are and all that you are made of."

"It's perfect," she said with a grin.

Rain exhaled slowly and began to head towards her new home and her new life, enamored with the amazing body bestowed upon her. Even with all the lessons and real-life accounts from the older souls, the journey was still an unknown: scary but also exciting. Rain landed gently on her new planet and began to run before her feet touched the ground. She could feel the warm, solid earth beneath her hoofs, and the tickle of the long grasses on her legs as she blissfully trotted on and on.

3

The Pegasus ran and ran, only slowing down when she spotted a group of horses in the distance who were peacefully sipping water from an overflowing creek.

Head held high, Rain strutted over to them with her wings outstretched proudly and offered warm hellos.

"What a glorious day it is to be alive on this Earth! How amazing to be a horse who can run and frolic and drink water from this cool creek!"

The other horses stopped drinking and tilted their heads in Rain's direction. Confused about what they saw, they exchanged glances and waited for the Alpha to respond.

"Well, yes, it is glorious to be a horse, but you are certainly not one!" the Alpha sputtered.

"What? Of course, I am!" Rain answered.

"You most definitely are not! You have big white wings! Horses do not have wings. Never did and never will!" the Alpha shot back and began to laugh.

"Well, technically, I'm a Pegasus, but I am part horse! I have the same legs like you and the same mane. My neigh is just the same as yours!" Rain argued, and she let out a powerful neigh to prove her point.

But it was too late; by now, the rest of the horses had joined the Alpha, although they seemed slightly unsure of their decision to do so. The sound of unsteady laughter echoed across the land. They turned their backs to Rain, and as they began to walk away, she shouted to them, "WAIT! Where are you going?!"

"Away from you!" snickered the Alpha. "We stick to our own, and you should do the same. Part horse is not ALL horse. Go play with the birds. Maybe they won't care how different you are!" The Alpha shook her mane and disappeared over a grassy hill, the other horses following slowly behind her.

Rain stood there for a few minutes, eyes closed, allowing the sounds of the gurgling brook to soothe her and help her to let go of the pain she felt. Eventually, the hurt subsided, and she was able to hold her head up high and shrug it off. "Oh well, I guess that's what having 'hurt feelings' feels like. It's actually not as bad as the teacher made it seem," she chuckled, thinking that the teacher and the Creator had been overly dramatic in their warnings. "It's not that big of a deal. Really. Besides, it's their loss not mine. I don't need them anyway because I can still fly!"

And with that thought in her mind, Rain took off running, faster and faster, flapping her wings harder and harder until, finally, she lifted off the ground and began soaring high above the trees. The breeze was warm yet felt cool against her feathers, and soon the young soul felt happy again.

After a while, Rain came upon a group of birds settled in the highest branches of the tallest tree, and felt convinced that the birds were with whom she belonged, the ones who would accept her, and be her family. Rain tried, again and again, to land in the tree beside them. Unfortunately, she was way too big for this and managed only to break some branches and disrupt the birds who flew into the sky, chirping and flapping angrily.

"WHAT ARE YOU DOING?!" they shrieked.

"I am a bird just like you are!" Rain answered back. "I just wanted to rest in the branches with you."

"You are no bird!" they yelled back. "You are much too big to be a bird, and you have four legs!"

"Well, technically, I'm a Pegasus," she explained again. "But I am part bird! I have soft feathers like you, and I can glide on the wind as you do," the young soul insisted.

"False! You are way more of a horse than you are a bird! You should go be with them." Then, like the horses, the birds flew off, leaving a sad and lonely young soul behind.

Rain was discouraged but still not ready to give up on finding her forever family. The young soul remembered the words of the Creator and the commitment that she had made. Her thoughts shifted to what the horses and birds had said. Thinking long and hard about everything, Rain decided that they were probably just puzzled by her appearance, and perhaps it was her approach that had been wrong. The young soul, soothed by this fact, decided to keep her wings down at first, so the next creature she came across wouldn't be confused by them. Rain knew that if they got the chance to know her, they wouldn't care that she was different.

So, the young soul set off on foot to find some new friends. The land was barren, but she marched along, determined and proud.

Finally, in the distance, she saw a giraffe. After she gave herself a quick pep talk, Rain walked right up to the giraffe and tried again to connect. "Hello, up there! It must be so great to be so tall and be able to reach so high!"

The giraffe stopped eating the tree's lush leaves and looked down lazily at Rain.

"What are you?" the giraffe managed to ask in-between bites.

"What do you mean? Isn't it obvious? I'm a horse!" Rain lied, pulling her wings in even tighter.

"No, you're not. You have feathers. Horses have hair, not feathers."

The young soul stretched out her wings. "Okay, fine. Then I'm a bird," she fibbed again.

"No, you're not. You have hooves instead of claws and no beak."

Rain's heart started racing, and her cheeks turned hot and red. "UGH! I'm a Pegasus, okay?" A bird AND a horse. Why does that matter so much, anyway? Who cares?"

"It's just how it is," replied the giraffe, becoming increasingly bored with the conversation. "We all stick to our 'own' kind; it's how it's always been. I have no idea where you fit in, but try the monkeys. They're not as smart as the rest of us. They might not care that you're different or even notice at all," the giraffe suggested, as it turned away from Rain and continued eating its delicious afternoon snack.

With a long sigh, the young soul refolded her wings, hung her head, and walked away slowly, her feet dragging and her heart heavy.

"Good luck, strange creature," the giraffe called out after Rain.

As Rain trudged along, she thought about her choice of form once again. *Was it a mistake? Should I have just been a bird or just been a horse? But how could I? I am so attached to both; they are both a part of me. There was never a choice. Still, what kind of life can I have, feeling so alone?* Rain wanted to believe that being true to herself, to what she felt in her heart, was the right thing, but found that convincing herself of this was getting harder and harder to do.

The young soul was so deep in thought that she didn't notice the monkeys until she heard them laughing. She looked up and saw them pointing and shouting in her direction.

"Horid!!! HORID ... HORRRRRIIIDDDDD."

Rain was confused at first, knowing she was familiar with the word but not remembering how, until it hit her. Horid. Horse bird. How was it possible that these monkeys could take the word that she had almost chosen to represent herself and make it sound so ugly and hurtful?

It's just a word, the young soul kept saying to herself. *It's just a word.*

Unfortunately, no matter how many times she said it, it still hurt just as much. They hadn't even let her get close enough to say hello, never mind give her a chance to explain, a chance to show them who she really was on the inside. They began to throw chunks of moss at her as if the name-calling wasn't bad enough. Rain, stunned by this level of cruelty, just stood there in disbelief for such a long time that she found herself almost entirely covered by it, the moss clinging to her back and wings.

"Perfect," Rain said out loud to no one in particular. "Now, I'll never fit in with anyone."

Seeing what the monkeys had done to the Pegasus made them laugh even harder.

"HAHAHA! Nice moss coat," yelled one, "MOSS COAT!" chimed the rest.

As Rain let the words sink in, she was suddenly struck with a brilliant idea.

If I have this moss all over me, no one will be able to see my wings, and then I can be with the horses. They'll never know I'm different! she thought to herself. The young soul knew it was a long shot, but she couldn't think of any other options, so she headed back the way she had come, moss coat and all.

First, Rain passed by the giraffe, who smiled and nodded in her direction.

"Well, hello there, young horse. What a lovely day for a stroll."

"Why, yes, it is!" replied Rain, pleased that her disguise had fooled the giraffe.

Continuing on, she came across the birds who whistled and chirped pleasantries at her. It was becoming increasingly clear that her plan might actually work.

After what seemed like forever, Rain saw the horses grazing ahead. She puffed her chest out, lifted her head high like she had not a care in the world, and trotted confidently towards them. A few of the horses looked up from their meals, but most just kept eating, undisturbed by her presence.

The Alpha walked over to Rain and extended a warm welcome.

"Hello, young horse, and where have you migrated from?"

Rain hesitated for a second and then responded. "Up North."

"Oh, yes. Yes, of course, the North. And this moss on your back is for?"

"To keep me warm, of course. Everyone in the North wears it," Rain responded matter-of-factly.

"Oh, right. Obviously," snorted the Alpha, acting familiar with the practice, unaware that it was all a farce. Assuming that the young horse was unique and full of confidence because she was a popular creature where she came from, the Alpha did something she rarely did. She asked Rain to join the group.

"We can always use some fresh blood and new ideas in our group, and if you don't have any pressing plans, we would love to have you stay with us."

Rain grinned from ear to ear, finally hearing the words she had longed to hear. As excited as she was, the young soul knew that to keep the act up, she'd have to play it cool.

"I suppose I can hang around for a while, I'm not expected anywhere right away," she said nonchalantly even though on the inside, she was dancing.

4

AND SO IT WAS, EVERY morning Rain would visit the monkeys and allow them to verbally taunt her and throw moss at her to cover her wings. If it meant she could finally belong to a group, the young soul felt that this demeaning act was worth it. She was happy, or at least she thought she was. Rain had a family now; she was indeed part of something.

A few weeks had passed, and Rain was fitting in quite nicely with the other horses. While she found their routine rather monotonous (eat, run, eat, run some more, sleep, repeat), she was grateful for it because it allowed her to maintain her routine with the monkeys. That was how it was; until one dreary afternoon, a bit of commotion in the woods caught her attention. She wandered over to the edge of the forest and saw three of the larger horses walking over with a smaller one.

The Alpha's voice boomed from behind her. "Well, well, and what do we have here?"

Rain turned and saw the rest of the herd coming up to join her.

"What's going on? Who is that?" she asked the horse next to her.

"That's Charlotte," she whispered back. "She used to live with us."

"Used to? What happened?"

"I think she just wanted to find her 'own' kind," the horse said, shrugging.

"Her 'own' kind? But she's a horse, no?"

"HA! Um, no. She's a PONY, and we are MUSTANGS."

"Oh," Rain said, confused. "Well, what's the difference? What's a pony?"

The horse sighed, annoyed by Rain's ignorance.

"A pony is a LITTLE horse. They're not as smart as we are. They can't run as fast."

Before Rain could ask another question, the three horses and the pony were upon them.

"Hello, Charlotte," the Alpha said smugly.

"It's Charlie," the pony countered.

"Right … Charlie," the horses snickered.

"Why are they laughing?" Rain whispered.

"Because Charlie is a BOY'S name, and she is a GIRL. Now, be quiet so I can hear."

Rain kept quiet but was more confused than ever. *Who cares what her name is?* she thought.

"So, what brings you back here, CHARLIE? Couldn't hack it out there in the wild all alone?" the Alpha snorted, her head held up high with arrogance.

"I handled it just fine," Charlie said. "I just …"

"Just what?"

"Just wanted to come back, is all."

The horses whispered amongst themselves, their

feelings on the matter not entirely clear.

"Hush, now," the Alpha said to them. "I pride myself on my compassion," she began. Rain shook her head gently, knowing all too well how untrue this statement was. "We will let her come back." The Alpha paused, and the horses scoffed.

"Thank you—" the pony began.

"I wasn't finished," the Alpha interrupted. "As I was saying, we will let you come back, but there will be conditions for your return."

Charlie sighed, "Of COURSE there's a catch; it's never easy with you."

"WHAT?! I'm offended!" the Alpha sputtered dramatically. "Considering you just walked away without so much as a goodbye, you should be ecstatic that we are even discussing this! We were so worried about you; it affected everyone."

The Alpha certainly knew how to put on a show. Rain had to give her credit for that.

But Charlie wasn't falling for it either.

"Riiiight, I'm sure you were," she said with an eye roll. "What are the conditions?"

The Alpha thought for a moment. "Well, first off, you will be permanently in charge of finding new grazing areas. Secondly, you will be permanently in charge of finding new watering holes. And thirdly ... um, thirdly ... you ... well, I can't think of a thirdly right now, so we'll just leave it as you owe me."

"Owe you?"

"US! I mean, you owe us; all of us, since you hurt us so dearly."

Charlie rolled her eyes again. "That's crazy! You know I'd have to do those things at night, and it will take the WHOLE night to accomplish! I will be tired all the time and have to sleep all day!!"

"Well, those are the conditions. You can always change your mind and go back out on your own, you know, since it was fine and all."

Charlie sighed. She knew she was beaten. "Fine. For now, I will do those things, but not forever. Once I've 'paid my dues,' we will revisit this conversation."

"Yeah, sure. Whatever," the Alpha said, half listening.

"Well, you better get some rest because your duties start tonight."

And with that, the conversation was over. The Alpha turned and walked off with her typical arrogant flare, and the rest of the group followed hesitantly, still unsure of how they felt about what had happened. Rain alone stayed behind.

"Hi, I'm Rain," she said gently.

"Charlie," she answered, "You're new, huh?"

"Yeah, I've only been here for a few weeks."

"And how are you liking it so far?"

"Well, they're my family now, so …"

Charlie laughed. "Yeah, some family. So, what's with all that moss all over your back?"

"Uh, I'm from up North; they all wear it up there."

"Huh, that's odd. I've been up North and never saw that before," Charlie challenged.

"You probably didn't notice. Anyway," Rain said, trying to change the subject, "why did you leave?"

"Eh, most of the horses here are okay, but they cower to the Alpha, and she and I never got along. They can be petty and cruel, and her three minions are even worse. She thinks I'm beneath her because I'm 'just a pony,' and she never misses an opportunity to remind me of it. She's just a bully."

"What's a bully?"

"You don't know what a bully is? How lucky you are! A bully is someone who picks on you and hurts your feelings because they're bigger or stronger or think they're better than you. It's someone who purposely tries to hurt your feelings and make you feel bad. Somehow that seems to make them feel better about themselves."

"Oh," Rain replied, knowing all too well what a bully was. Now, she finally had the word to describe it.

"Yeah, she tried to kick me out in the beginning because she said I was too different, but we're both a breed of horse, so she couldn't."

"I am a breed of horse, and she kicked me out too!" Rain blurted out unintentionally.

"Wait. What? What are you talking about? You're definitely a horse, and you haven't been kicked out because you're here, right?"

Rain, terrified that she just ruined everything and that her secret would be out, tried intently to come up with a justifiable response.

"I mean because I'm the only white horse here. Uh, she was going to kick me out, but I uh … um … never mind. It was a while ago and silly; no need to relive the past."

"Uh, yeah. Okay," Charlie agreed, but she knew something seemed off about her. "Anyway, I better go rest before my new 'jobs' start." She walked off, shaking her head, annoyed about the conditions of her return.

A few days later, Rain bumped into Charlie as she was coming back from finding the latest watering hole. While it seemed like an easy task, these little lakes tended to dry up or become overcrowded quickly, so they were always on the hunt for new ones.

"Hey, Charlie!" Rain exclaimed

"HA! Well, aren't you in a chipper mood."

"Well, yes, of course! Why wouldn't I be?"

"Guess there's no reason for you not to be, you know, since you have no responsibilities and can do whatever you want," Charlie mumbled tiredly.

"If you hate it so much here, then why do you stay?" Rain asked gently.

Charlie sighed. "It's not that I hate it here; it just seems silly that I have to do all of this like I'm being punished for wanting to see what else is out there."

"Why did you come back really?" Rain pressed.

"It's hard out there and lonely. I left because I wanted to find more of my kind, honestly. I know I said I am a horse, and I fought the Alpha on it to stay, but I'll never be truly accepted here, not like everyone else. I'll always be different. I couldn't find any other ponies, and the other species out there are even less accepting than the horses. So, I just figured, better to be part of a dysfunctional family than part of none at all."

"Yeah, I know what you mean," Rain said with a heavy heart.

Charlie tilted her head and stared intensely into Rain's eyes for what felt like forever. Rain started to fidget, hoping she hadn't given herself away again, preparing for all the questions she couldn't answer, but Charlie remained silent.

"Anyway, this won't be forever," Charlie continued, "The Alpha is just trying to prove a point. My buddies are going to talk to her, and hopefully, this will all be over soon. So, I have to suck it up for now."

"Yeah, totally," Rain said, breathing a sigh of relief, her secret still locked away.

"Well, I'm going to go eat and rest, but if you're up for it later, would you wanna come with me tonight? I'll be looking for a new pasture. Pretty exciting stuff! I know you'd just hate to miss it!" she laughed.

While Charlie initially invited Rain for her company, she knew that this radiant white horse was hiding something, and she was desperate to know what it was. Perhaps, if she found out Rain's secret, she could tell the others, win them over, and get out of doing these time-consuming chores.

As soon as the thought had entered Charlie's head, it quickly became her mission: find the secret and free herself. Unfortunately, the more time she spent with Rain, the more she began to like her. They had become as close as sisters, and she cherished the time they spent together. When the day finally came that Charlie found out Rain's secret, she had already forgotten about her plan to use it to get herself into the Alpha's good graces.

It was a warm spring afternoon when the two headed out on yet another trek; this time to find dandelions, a spring treat for the horses and another chore that the Alpha had added to Charlie's list. They were chatting and laughing, having a grand old time when they happened to find a watering hole hidden by the woods.

"Ohh, it's warm out. Let's take a break and have a swim!" suggested Charlie, and without another word, she jumped right in.

"Um, yeah. I'm kind of cold. I'll wait out here," Rain said hesitantly.

"Oh, please! It's not cold out, and the water's so warm!"

"Yeah. No thanks! I don't want to get wet," she said, practically begging her friend to leave it alone.

Charlie just shrugged and swam around, splashing Rain in jest.

"Stop! Don't do that!" Rain shouted, her body trembling with panic.

"Why not? I'm just playing around! What's the problem? Are you allergic to water all of a sudden?" she laughed, splashing her, again and again. Rain did her best to get out of the way, but it was too late. Some of the moss had slid off her body, exposing her feathers.

"What the—" Charlie stared at her in disbelief. "Are those feathers? DO YOU HAVE WINGS?" she yelled.

"SHHHHHH," Rain pleaded. "Please, be quiet. Please."

Charlie stopped splashing and grew silent, realizing the dangers of the secret Rain carried around with her.

"If they find out," Charlie whispered and shook her head, her eyes wide with fright.

"You don't have to tell them; I'll just leave. You can say you don't know where I went, that I just disappeared," Rain pleaded as she began to walk away.

"What? Wait? Where are you going?"

"Away. On my terms, not theirs."

"Stop being so dramatic," Charlie said, "I'm not going to tell anyone."

"You're not?"

"Of course not! You're my sister, silly. Your secret is

safe with me!"

"Really?" Rain asked, hopefully. "You don't care that I'm not one hundred percent horse?"

"Yeah. Really. And I'm not one hundred percent horse either, so who am I to judge?" Charlie said, chuckling.

"Under one condition, of course," she said in her best Alpha voice.

Rain relaxed a little and smiled at her friend's joke. "And what condition would that be?"

"You have to tell me what you are and let me see your wings!"

"Oh, I don't know ..."

"What don't you know? I know, and you know, so we both know. The secret is out, so just let me see already!"

"Fine ... My form is called a Pegasus—part bird, part horse," Rain said, walking into the pond to slowly shed herself of the moss. It felt so good that she closed her eyes and stretched out her wings; they were sore from being held so tight against her all the time. She felt free.

Charlie watched her in awe. "I know when I chose to be a pony, all I wanted was to be a horse, but they seemed too big and intrusive. How did you ever decide to be a Pegasus? I didn't even know that was an option!"

"Well, I felt connected to the birds and the horses. I wanted to soar through the sky and race on land. I never knew it existed either until I went to where the lights were dim." Rain took a deep breath and told Charlie what happened with the grey soul and her teacher.

"Wow," Charlie said after a moment. "That's quite a story! Knowing what you know now, do you regret your decision?"

"Sometimes ... most times." Rain paused, trying to find the right words to help her friend understand. "It's like I got what I wanted; I am who I believe myself to be, but to be accepted, I have to hide it. So, these wings that I love so dearly have become a curse, and I find myself thinking it would almost be better without them," she said, finishing with a sigh.

"I understand what you're saying," Charlie said sadly. "It must be difficult to feel torn in two different directions like that."

Rain shrugged almost a little too vigorously like she was trying to shake the pain out of her heart.

"Do you ever get to fly?"

"Oh, no! I'd love to, but I just can't risk it."

"What a waste!" Charlie exclaimed. "If I had wings, I'd fly everywhere!"

"Yeah, right! You barely get to be with the group just because you went out in the world; I can only imagine what they would do if they caught me FLYING!"

"HA! That's the truth! But ... that doesn't mean you can't do it at all! You just need to be smart about it."

Charlie thought about that for a minute.

"Wait, I've got it! You can fly at night!"

"What? No way! I'll get caught, and then forced to leave."

"Nah. You come out with me all the time anyway! And you know they always go to bed and get up at the same time every day. No one is going to suspect anything! They never cared before! It's the PERFECT plan!"

"I don't know," Rain said hesitantly.

"Here we go again with the 'I don't know.' Tonight, you will fly, and it will be wonderful."

Rain sighed. "Maybe."

"Maybe, schmaybe," Charlie scoffed. "It's happening. You've been trapped down on this soil for far too long; it's time to get some use out of those—YES!" she exclaimed, struck with an idea. "You can fly high above the trees and help me find dandelions! It will make my job soooo much easier."

Rain chuckled "Well, as long as it helps you out!"

"Yup, got that right," Charlie smiled.

Rain smiled back, knowing that her friend had spun the situation, making it seem like she was doing Charlie a favor, making it easier for her to accept.

Later that evening, Rain spread her wings for the first time in months and took to the sky. She felt the crisp spring air flow through her feathers once again and experienced a bliss she had been missing for so long.

5

THE YOUNG SOUL FINALLY HAD a group of close friends, and Charlie had become like a sister to her. She had peers to eat, drink, play, laugh, and rest with, everything she had ever desired. She went out with Charlie and spread her wings almost every night without the horses suspecting a thing. While her secret life remained a secret, something still didn't feel right.

After a while, her secret began to take its toll. It wasn't enough that Charlie knew anymore; she also wanted to be honest with the rest of her friends too. She was tired of sneaking around, but her fear of rejection kept her quiet. Charlie had accepted her unconditionally and encouraged her to be herself, but she wasn't sure the others would feel the same, especially with the ever-opinionated Alpha in the lead. Rain knew that the hot summer months were almost upon her since the "moss coat" grew warmer by the day. Soon, it all became too much, and Rain couldn't bear it any longer.

One particularly humid day, the young soul snuck away to swim at the hidden watering hole that she and Charlie had found months ago. Feeling safe there, Rain shook her wings, quickly shedding the moss that clung to her, and waded into the cool water. She was splashing around, having a blast, until she heard the sound of neighing; she instantly froze. Rain slowly turned and came face-to-face with her "family," who was looking down at her with disgust and anger.

"What? What's wrong?" the young soul asked meekly, pushing her wings deeper into the water, trying to figure out how to play it off. She was completely caught off guard because it was during this time the horses usually napped. Their broken routine seemed planned and suspicious.

"WHAT'S WRONG??" shouted the Alpha "YOU!! YOU are what's wrong. You're an IMPOSTER! I knew that I recognized you from somewhere. We've met before, haven't we? You're that weird bird-horse animal! The Pega-something! We made it clear that you weren't welcome here because you are NOT one of us. You are no longer part of this family. Stay away, for good! I never want to see your face around here again!!"

With that, the Alpha dramatically turned away and strutted off with the rest of the horses following hesitantly behind.

"WAIT!" Rain called out after them, "I am the same as I was before! You are my family. You liked who I was on the inside, so it shouldn't matter what I look like on the outside!"

A few of the horses turned back to look at the young soul, pity written all over their resolute faces.

"We're sorry," one of them said with a sad look in his eyes, "But the Alpha is right. We must stick to our own, even if we don't always agree. It's better to be in a group than left all alone." With heads hung low, they too walked off. Only Charlie was left.

"I'm so, so sorry," she began.

"IT WAS YOU?!" Rain shouted as the fog that surrounded her brain began to dissipate. "It had to be you. No one else even knows this place exists! You told them my secret! But why? Why would you do that?! What could have possibly made it worth it?"

Charlie remained silent.

"You got … you got out of all your extra jobs! Is that it? You gave me up so that you didn't have to do all that work anymore! AM I RIGHT?" Rain screamed.

"No way. I mean, yes. Before I got to know you, that was the plan, but then—" Charlie said, trying to answer.

"Go away!!" Rain said, not wanting to hear her explanation.

"YOU DON'T UNDERSTAND! IT'S NOT WHAT YOU THINK!" Charlie shouted back, frustrated, and wanting to be heard.

"I don't care. I thought we were friends … sisters. Apparently, I was wrong, and nothing you say is going to change that."

Charlie held her ground and tried again to speak. "Rain, listen to me, I had no CHOICE. I—"

"GET OUT OF HERE! I DON'T WANT TO SEE YOUR LYING FACE," Rain shouted at the top of her lungs. "You've become what you hate the most, a BULLY. You told me to fly, and then you shot me down! Get away from me." Rain spun around so Charlie couldn't see her tears. "I don't need you, anyway. I don't need anyone," Rain said, attempting to convince them both.

Her heart was broken, and her family destroyed. It took her a few minutes to calm down, but by the time she turned back around, ready to give Charlie a chance to explain, she had left. Eventually, the young soul dragged herself out of the water and headed off, away from the place she thought she'd spend the rest of her life.

After walking for what felt like weeks, the air began to turn cold, and tiny beads of ice began to form on her wings. Rain kept on as white powder that made her hooves quiver slowly replaced the warm ground. *This must be snow*, she thought. The snow was something she had heard the horses speak of and something that she had pretended to be familiar with, part of the act she had to keep up with since she was "from the North."

The powder grew thicker and thicker, leading up to an icy body of water. Rain smelled it before she saw it, the cold breeze ringing with the salty odor of the sea. It was the largest body of water she had ever seen, and she stood there mesmerized by it, barely noticing that she was shivering. She thought about how the moss blanket would have come in handy here and chuckled to herself as she noted the irony.

Her hooves seemed to slip and slide on the ground, so she made sure to stop carefully when she finally reached the edge of the ocean. Lowering her face to the water, she attempted to take a much-needed sip as her journey had left her quite thirsty, but quickly spit the salty water out.

"That is terrible! What is wrong with this water?" she said out loud to herself. Unbeknownst to her, these words were carried deep into the sea, and no more than a few seconds later, a creature surfaced who would change everything for her. Startled, as she believed herself to be alone in this frozen place, Rain instinctively hid her wings, which she had been mindlessly fluffing against her body to provide warmth. The instant Rain recognized the creature, she felt free to relax. It was a narwhal!

"Hello, there!" she began excitedly, feeling more confident than she had in a long time.

The narwhal looked at her. It bobbed in and out of the water with only its horn visible at times.

Rain tried again. "You're a narwhal! I've seen your form before, up in the sky! You're one of the mixed souls! I was told that to see one of your kind was almost impossible! Such luck!"

A clicking and a low buzzing sound were all that came from the majestic giant.

"I'm sorry! I don't understand. Can you speak? Do you know how?" Rain questioned.

"Of course I know how to speak," the narwhal shot back. "Just because I choose not to does not make me stupid."

"Oh no! I'm so sorry! I didn't mean to imply—"

"What do you want?" the narwhal demanded.

"Well, um ... Hi, my name is Rain. What's yours?"

"It doesn't matter."

"Okay … well, I thought maybe, since we are both mixed, that we could be friends? Maybe even family?"

"Don't use that word, 'mixed.' I don't like it; it's derogatory and offensive."

"I'm so sorry. I didn't mean to offend—I didn't know—"

"Why would you think that you and I could be friends?"

"Because we are both mixed—different. We can understand and support each other."

"You are right. We are both mixed—different. You live on land, and I live in the sea. You need the warmth, and I need the cold. Just because we are both different, doesn't make us the same."

Becoming increasingly discouraged, Rain tried a different approach.

"Are you all alone? Do you have a family? Are there other narwhals here or other sea creatures you spend your time with?"

"No."

Rain looked into the creature's eyes and patiently waited for him to continue.

The narwhal sighed. "Look, young soul, I don't mean to come across as insensitive or unfriendly, but I've spent most of my days here on Earth regretting the decision I made long ago to choose the form of a narwhal. It is a lonely existence, one I can't wait to be rid of. On occasion, I think about just giving up and going back early," he finished sadly.

"NO!! You can't do that!"

"And why not?"

"It's not good for your soul. You could be trapped up there forever, or disappear completely!"

"How could you possibly know that?"

"It's a long story, but trust me, it's the truth."

"I don't know anything about that, but even if it is true, sometimes being here all alone makes me feel like I have already disappeared."

The narwhal bobbed back into the calm waters, and Rain feared that her time with him had ended. The Pegasus waited a moment and then turned her back to the sea, saddened by the conversation but ready to forge ahead.

"Wait!" Rain heard over her shoulder.

"Oh! I thought you had gone."

"I must go, yes. A storm is brewing, and I must swim out to sea where it is safer. I wanted to say that you are right. It's not worth putting my soul in jeopardy just because I'm sad. It was my decision and mine alone, and I will do what I must to carry on until the Creator is ready to take me back. I have found staying away from others the best way to protect myself, as I have tried and failed at friendships many times over the years. Maybe it's time for me to give it another shot."

"I am glad to hear you say that you'll keep trying," Rain replied, forcing a smile. "Perhaps, one day, you will find a creature to love and who will love you back. Just please, don't ever give up."

"I wish you the same luck. Thank you for your kind words, and good luck on your journey. Stay open and be strong. I see happiness awaiting you."

And with that, the narwal ducked back under the water, and his horn vanished from sight.

As she walked cautiously back to warmer land, Rain thought about all that had happened to her and her options for moving forward. In Earth's time, it had been only a few years, but to Rain, it seemed like an eternity.

How much longer will the Creator keep me here? she wondered. *Weeks? Years? Decades?*

After a while, the Earth began to thaw and finally soften. She found herself at the border of a thick forest. The narwhal had told her to be open and strong, but she was tired, not just from her journey but from being rejected time and time again. Rain decided at that moment to live as the narwhal had; in solitude. She slowly headed towards the cover of the trees, her wings dragging on the ground.

I will live in the woods, where no one can see me or hurt me ever again.

And that's precisely what she did.

The days turned into weeks and the weeks into months. Rain kept to herself and avoided any and all contact with the other animals, convincing herself that this was for the best.

6

One warm spring day, after wandering around aimlessly, Rain found herself on the banks of a wide river. The young soul stood there fixated, watching the fast-moving water crash against smooth, grey rocks scattered haphazardly throughout the river. That was until a strange reflection caught her eye. Rain looked up and found herself face-to-face with a majestic elephant. She recognized its form from her time in the sky. The two creatures stood frozen with amazement, staring at each other quietly for what seemed like hours, Rain especially mesmerized by this massive creature with it's small, kind eyes.

Finally, the elephant spoke. "Hello, beautiful soul. My name is Ellie. What's yours?"

"Rain," the young soul softly responded as she tucked her wings in closer.

The elephant tilted her head curiously. "Why are you trying to hide your wings?"

"I don't know what you're talking about," Rain snorted back.

Rain turned away with a huff and a shake of her mane, walking briskly into the cover of the woods. All of that time, she had spent alone, and her past experiences had made her bitter and untrusting; majestic creature or not, she was not going to allow herself to be hurt again.

Unfortunately, Rain's determination to live a solitary life wasn't as easy as she had imagined. Late one crisp fall evening, she was pacing back and forth in the small clearing she now called home. This is something she often did, as it calmed her. Thick oak trees flanked the clearing. In-between two of the largest trees, Rain had built herself a small structure that provided shelter from the rain and sun. More importantly, it kept her hidden from any other creatures that should happen to pass by. It took her weeks to collect fallen branches and leaves, a process that would have been much easier had she used her wings. She found it easy to blame all her hardships on her wings, and so she continued to do so. Over time, she began to hate them and pretended that they didn't exist. She was ashamed of them, as well as many of her past choices.

Every day she followed the same routine: wake up,

pace the clearing, find food, go to the nearby river to drink, go back to her clearing, pace some more, and rest. She repeated the same things throughout the day. She perked her ears, always listening for any sound that would give away a nearby animal. Upon hearing anything, she would run into her home and wait for them to pass. More often than not, the sounds she heard were rustling leaves or the occasional chipmunk scampering by. After a while, she became less and less jumpy, slowly letting down her guard, convinced that after such a long time, no creatures would pass by. And none had, until that fateful fall evening.

It started out as a quiet sound that she identified as the wind or possibly a squirrel. She quickly dismissed it. Then she heard another, and another, and by the time she realized that this could actually be something, it was too late. Moments later, she found herself face-to-face with a zebra. Rain immediately recognized zebras from the dimly-lit room up in the stars. Her initial reaction to its presence was one of happiness, yet she was quickly reminded of her conversation with the narwhal, and her mood shifted to a more somber place. Rain stood motionless, wings clenched tight against her body, holding her breath as if it would cause her to become invisible. Neither one of them spoke.

The zebra was young and looked lost and scraggly, as though it hadn't eaten or slept in days.

Finally, he collapsed on the ground, overtaken by sheer exhaustion. Rain took pity on the zebra and carefully dragged him into her home. She went out, found him food, and coaxed him to eat it. She covered him with moss to keep him warm and stood by his side day and night. This became her new routine, slowly bringing him back to life as he fell in and out of consciousness. This situation suited her well. She was happy to take care of someone else, to have company, even if the relationship was at the moment, one-sided. But it made her afraid as well.

She thought, *What if he gets better and hates me or thinks I'm an abomination, or even worse, leaves me?* she thought. After a few days, however, the zebra felt better and spoke his first words with a weak smile.

"My name is Zeek. What's yours?"

"Rain," she replied cautiously.

"Where am I?"

"Deep in the woods." That was the best answer she could give him.

"How did I get here? Where is my family? Where is your family?" The questions flowed quickly, as he tried unsuccessfully to stand up, becoming noticeably uneasy as the reality of his situation came into focus.

"Whoa, whoa! Slow down," Rain insisted. "I will tell you everything I know. You were very sick when you got here, and you're still recovering. You need to take it easy. You're safe here; there's no need to panic."

Zeek begrudgingly sat back down and waited for Rain to continue speaking.

"Well, actually, there's not much to tell; you stumbled into my home, weak and unwell, and so I took you in and nursed you back to health. As to what led you here in the first place, I'm sorry, I'm really not sure."

"Oh," Zeek replied slowly as his memory came back to him, "I had a fight with someone in my family, and I ran away."

"What happened?"

"It's silly. Really. He was making fun of me for being short. He always makes fun of me for being short and not as good at doing things as he is."

Rain didn't say anything for a long time. She couldn't wrap her head around the fact that this creature was lucky enough to have a family, and yet CHOSE to leave them. She was mad and jealous, but she also knew this soul was not the same as she was, and most likely had a completely different life experience than she had. Zeek was a part of a loving family, one who wanted him, and as hard as she tried, she still wasn't accepted by anyone.

"I'm sorry you were so upset that you felt that you had to leave."

Zeek just shrugged, too tired to do anything else. "I should try to go back; they're probably worried."

"I don't know your family or where to find them, but I will help you look if you'd like."

"Really?"

"Of course, but we need to wait until you're completely

healed before we can travel very far," Rain cautioned.

"Yes, yes! Whatever you say! Thank you!" Zeek exclaimed, feeling better already.

For the next week or so, the two lived harmoniously. With every passing day, Zeek grew strong, and he began to help Rain gather food and keep the clearing free of fallen branches and leaves. Rain told herself not to get too comfortable in her current situation and kept reminding herself that soon he would be well enough to travel, and she'd be all alone once again. But keeping her heart at a safe distance proved to be harder than she thought. She found herself laughing at his silly jokes, and his presence provided her comfort at night when the Earth got dark and quiet. Finally, the day came when he was healthy enough to begin searching for his family, and Rain became quiet and sad. Zeek noticed her change in behavior and questioned her about it.

"I am excited for you to find your family, but I'm sad because it means you will no longer be here with me, and I'll be all alone," she confessed.

"What are you talking about? You'll live with us, of course! I will not leave you here by yourself!"

Rain shook her head. "Zeek, you do not understand. We are not the same species, and because of that, your family will probably not want me to live with them."

"That's silly! Of course, they will! You saved my life!"

"Yes, but that won't matter. We took opposite paths to

get to where we are, and those decisions will affect us now."

"You're wrong! You don't know them. They'll love you, I'm sure of it!" Zeek insisted.

Rain knew he was naïve, but she didn't want to continue arguing with him. So, she did what she thought was best and ended the conversation with a smile and a nod.

Every morning they would go out in a different direction, hoping to come across Zeek's family or at least a trail to locate them. Every night they would return home and tell themselves that tomorrow would be the day that they would finally find them. Zeek spent those days chattering away, telling Rain all about his family and friends, detailing all of the things they were going to do together when they finally reunited. While Rain tried not to get her hopes up, the thought crept into her head that maybe he was right; perhaps they would welcome her with open arms.

Day after day, they searched, and once they had gone out in every direction, they started all over again, staying out later and later, covering more ground than they had the first time around. Yet, as the days wore on, they both became increasingly discouraged. It was Zeek who finally called off the search.

They were finishing breakfast one morning when he said matter-of-factly, "I don't want to look for them anymore."

While Rain had seen this coming, she was surprised that it had happened so soon. "But it's only been a few weeks; there are still places we can look."

"No. We have looked long enough. If my family wanted to find me, they would be looking too, and there has been no trace of them. I am tired of wandering around. It's time to move on and accept the truth that they're lost to me forever."

"Well, you're more than welcome to stay here with me. It's not much, but we can make it work. We've done okay so far," Rain responded gently, feeling guilty over her excitement to finally have a permanent companion.

"I'd really like to stay here with you; it'll be great. We can be each other's family."

And, so it was.

They spent their days enjoying the woods instead of searching them, and their nights looking up at the stars, pointing out shapes, and inventing stories about them. During one of their walks, they ended up at the same fast-moving river where Rain had found herself once before. While Zeek bent over to take a sip of the cool water, Rain looked across the way and saw the same elephant that she had seen long ago. The elephant stood among the trees, watching them silently, motioning with her long trunk towards a large rock close to Rain. Confused, she looked over at the rock and saw a thin black object in the shape of a circle, a dried flower resting beside it. Not sure of what it was, or its purpose, Rain looked back up at the elephant for answers, but instead found herself hypnotized by the creature's bright blue eyes once again. After a few long seconds, she shook herself free and told Zeek it was time to go, completely forgetting about the circle on the rock. As they walked away, she looked over her shoulder, but the elephant had disappeared back into the forest.

That night, as they sat in front of the fire, Rain decided to ask Zeek about his journey to Earth. It was something that had been on her mind for some time. Since he was going to be around for a while, she felt like it was finally okay to ask.

"Zeek," she began, "I couldn't help but notice that you are a young zebra. How small were you when you landed? What was it that made you choose to be a zebra?"

Zeek looked at Rain with a puzzled expression. "Well, I was born a baby, of course! I came from my parents as all the animals do! And what do you mean to choose? I didn't have a choice; I am the same as my parents."

"Wow, how interesting," Rain replied. "Not me. I came to Earth fully grown, and I chose to be a Pegasus ..." she said, trailing off as she thought about the decision that she made all those years ago.

"Wait. Really? My family often told stories of our distant relatives choosing to be zebras and arriving on Earth fully grown, but we thought they were just making it up!"

"What did they say?" Rain questioned excitedly.

Zeek jumped up, startling Rain, and danced around the fire. He had a flair for the dramatic and was never one to miss out on an opportunity to tell a good story.

"Well," he began, "many, many, moons ago, my great-great-great-great-GREAT grandpa's soul lived in a big beautiful universe. He had many friends up there, but he wanted more, so he decided to come to Earth. This was back when the Earth had just been formed. He wanted to be a horse but have stripes like the mighty tiger. So, the Creator made him a majestic zebra."

Rain leaned in close like any good audience member would, acting as if she was hanging onto his every word.

"Then, he came down to Earth." Zeek pranced back and forth, demonstrating the descent.

This time Rain laughed out loud. "You are quite the storyteller!" she commented.

"Thanks!" he exclaimed.

"And then what happened?" she asked.

"And thennnnn ... he wandered around until he found my great-great-great-great-GREAT grandma, and they fell in love and had babies, and the rest is history!" He finished with a curtsy and a bow of his head.

"Is it all true? Those tales they told us?" Zeek asked, "Is that how your story goes too? I've never met anyone who had chosen their form and come down all grown up before."

"Hmmm," Rain said, unsure of how to answer. "Well, my story is similar to your great-great-gr—your many great grandpas, but also different. When I was up in the universe, it was wonderful, and I too had many friends, but there were also teachers."

"Teachers for what?"

"Well, to teach us about the ways of the universe and prepare us for our time on Earth. They also helped us choose our forms."

"Ohhh, tell me everything!" Zeek urged excitedly. "How many creatures were up there? How did you ever choose?!"

Rain laughed at the irony. Here was this zebra so interested in learning about the one thing that she was always trying to forget. But there was no way he could possibly understand her feelings about that decision. Zeek had been born to a loving family, one who wanted him and aspired to create him, and he had no attachment to any form, in particular, so he'd never have to fight for his choice, or deal with the consequences of it. But Rain couldn't think of a good enough reason not to be honest with him about it. So, she took a deep breath and started from the beginning.

She told him about the light rooms and the dark ones, and her struggle to choose her form. She told him about the grey soul and the conversation with her teacher. She told him about her time on Earth and her struggles and pitfalls. When she finally finished speaking, Zeek just stared at her, mesmerized.

"That is a very different story then what I've heard," he finally spoke. "I wonder how long it took my great-great-great-great-GREAT grandpa to find my grandma. I wonder if he was sad and lonely like you were before he did."

"I don't know, but in the end, it all worked out, and that's all that matters," Rain said. "I am still confused about how you came to Earth as a baby and didn't get a choice in the matter ..."

"Oh, right!" Zeek exclaimed. "I forgot that part ... so, the story goes that back in the old days ... like old, old days, there were only a few species of animals, so all souls got to choose. Eventually, more and more souls chose the same form and were able to have babies."

"Wait, what's a baby?" asked Rain.

"Um ... a baby is a tiny creature that looks like its mom and dad; it cries and spits and can't do anything for itself."

"How do you have them?"

Zeek shrugged. "Don't know. I never had one. I asked once, and it was something about birds and bees and being in love."

"Interesting," Rain said curiously. "And you don't get to choose your form if you come as a baby?"

"I guess not. I guess my mom and dad decided for me. All I know is that I don't remember being in the sky like you, or having to choose anything. One day, I was just here."

"Did you like it?"

"Like what?"

"Being a baby?"

Zeek laughed. "I don't know! I don't remember all that. My family has all sorts of stories about us from when we were babies. I think they made some of them up just to tease us."

"What kind of stories?"

"My brother says I was born with no stripes, and they had to paint them on, and my cousin tells everyone that I used to cry every time it rained, but I don't believe that for a second because I'm tough."

"What's a brother and a cousin?" Rain questioned.

"Uh, well, my mom and dad had other babies besides me, and they're my brothers and sisters. My mom and dad's brothers and sisters—they're called aunts and uncles—had babies, and they're my cousins."

"Wow! How many people are in your family?" Rain asked, a hint of jealousy visible in her voice.

"Ha!" Zeek snorted. "I have three brothers and two sisters and tons of aunts and uncles and cousins. Too many people, if you ask me, there is never any peace and quiet."

"Maybe, but how lucky you are to have a family, to have that many people around who love you, want to protect you, and travel through life with you."

"Yeah, it's cool, I guess," Zeek responded sadly.

"I'm sorry," she said, watching his smile disappear. "Did

I say something wrong?"

"No, I just never really thought of it like that. I kind of miss them."

"I know you do. You know, we can try looking for them again. Maybe they were going one way, and we were going the other! Yeah, I bet that's it!" Rain said brightly, trying to cheer him up.

"Nah, it's okay. I'm tired of looking. Besides, I like it here with you."

Rain could tell he was just pretending to be okay. "Well, it's probably better off that we just stay put anyway. That way, it'll be easier for them to find you."

"Sure, whatever you say. I'm tired. I'm going to bed. Night."

"Night, Zeek," she answered back. "Sleep well, little bell."

Zeek smiled at Rain's routine evening farewell and headed to bed.

Rain stared into the dwindling fire, her head full of questions. Zeek had given her so much information she didn't know where to start. It seemed as if all creatures had struggled at one time or another, and she couldn't make sense of the fact that their relatives, the creatures that now flourished, wouldn't be more accepting. Did they not know the history of their existence? Did they not know their ancestors' struggles, or did they just not care? *I'm on the same journey that so many others have been on before me, and yet it still hasn't gotten any easier,* Rain thought to herself. Their troubles are my troubles, and yet, they act as though they can't understand. Perhaps that's because it wasn't their journey. Maybe that's why this behavior continues; hearing a story about something so long ago is much different than actually living that life.

She was dizzy with questions but knew no one could answer them. There was no point. She vowed to shove the questions to the back of her head with all the others and just move forward. She was no longer all alone, and she should focus on that and be grateful.

When the last of the embers had grown cold, she too went to bed.

7

Life continued as weeks came and went. Zeek and Rain had built a more substantial, more comfortable dwelling for themselves, and they had settled into a happy existence.

One fall evening, they were resting inside when they heard the crunching of leaves nearby. Zeek had adopted Rain's caution of foreign noises, so this caused them both to freeze. The sound grew louder until it was right next to them. Zeek, who couldn't contain his curiosity any longer, jumped up and ran out of the dwelling. The next few seconds were filled with squeals of joy and happiness. Rain, concerned about Zeek and curious herself, finally stepped outside and found Zeek surrounded by a dazzle of zebras. Her heart dropped instantly. Zeek's family had found him. She stood there as an outsider in her own home, waiting to see what would happen, not sure what to do.

Zeek finally turned towards Rain and began to introduce her to his family, telling them how she saved his life and helped him search for them. If that wasn't enough, she then gave him a home when he felt hopeless and lost. The zebras looked at Rain, studying her closely.

"Thank you for saving our son. We've been looking for him for so long. We never gave up hope, and now I'm so glad we didn't. Thank you for keeping him safe. We are forever in your debt."

"See!!!" Zeek exclaimed. "I told you they would love you!"

Rain smiled, still too hesitant to get excited about the idea. "It's late. You must be tired from your journey. Are you hungry? Thirsty?"

"Oh, no, we're okay, but thank you!" Zeek's father answered. "We must be getting back now. We've been away for such a long time; it's time to go home."

"Oh, yeah. Sure, I understand," Rain whispered.

"Okay, let's go!" Zeek said as he began to lead the group out of the clearing. "Rain, come on! Let's gooooooo."

Rain didn't move.

"Oh, Zeek, honey. Rain can't come with us," soothed his mother.

"What?? Why not?"

"Well, because Rain is a horse who has wings, and we are zebras."

"So?"

"Zeek," Rain interrupted. "It's okay, I understand."

"What's to understand?" he retorted angrily.

"We're different," Rain said.

"But who cares? You saved me! You befriended me. Who cares that we're different on the outside!"

"Zeek, honey. Rain is right. Our kind started out like her, a creature with no family. While we understand her loneliness, we have worked too hard and waited too long to be accepted. We can't risk doing anything that could jeopardize that."

"Yeah, yeah. I KNOW all of that!! Which is why she should come with us! Wouldn't you have wanted great-great-great-great-GREAT grandpa to be taken in by someone else? This is so unfair!" Zeek whined.

"I know," his mom said. "Of course, we'd have wanted him to be accepted, but perhaps if he had been, he'd have never met your great-great-great-great-GREAT grandma, and none of us would be here! I'm sorry, honey, but it has to be this way. Please, say your goodbyes. It's time to go."

"NO!" Zeek shouted, stomping his hoof. "I'm staying here with Rain. If you want to leave me here, that's fine; but I'M not leaving her alone."

Rain moved closer to Zeek. "Dear friend, you mean the world to me, but you must go. You are lucky enough to have a family, and I cannot allow you to give that up, especially for me. I will be fine, and I'm sure we will meet one day again."

"But this … this just isn't right!"

Realizing that Zeek was facing a moral dilemma, Rain decided to make it easier for him.

"Just go! I never even wanted you here; I just felt bad for you, that's why I let you stay. LEAVE!!"

Zeek stood there, shocked by Rain's outburst.

"GO!!" Rain shouted, trying to disguise her tears with angry words. "Go now!"

The zebras stood quietly for a moment, watching to see what Zeek would do. He ran up to Rain and snuggled up against her.

"I will always remember you, whether you remember me or not."

With that, he turned and walked away, he, too, trying to hide his tears.

As Rain watched the zebras walk away, nuzzling Zeek, welcoming him back to the family, she was emotionless. She had nothing left to feel. *That is the last straw,* she told herself. *No more. I'm not going to try anymore. I'm not going to let anyone in ever again. I just don't care. Being alone isn't so bad,* she thought. *Eventually, I'll go back and choose a new soul, an easy, well-known, accepted one, just like my teacher and Creator had suggested.*

For days, Rain moped around, doing only what she

needed to do to keep herself fed and comfortable, waiting for the day the Creator would take her back. That would have been a fine way to live for some, but Rain's spirit was just too big for this sad, lonely life, and she knew it. She was continually trying to come up with ideas of how to lead a normal existence, even though her heart wasn't in it anymore. Choosing a new form right now was out of the question, but maybe there was a way she could permanently change hers somehow. And then it struck her! If she got rid of her wings, she'd be a horse and only a horse. While she was excited about her solution, she knew the execution was going to be tricky.

First, she tried spreading her wings out and running multiple times into a thick tree, hoping they'd just rip off, but her only success had come in the form of scrapes, bruises, and, eventually, exhaustion. Rain took a break and sat under the shade of the tree, trying to figure out how else to get rid of her wings. Perhaps, she could cut them off, but what would she use?

She got up and began wandering around the forest, looking for something sharp and sturdy but found nothing. Eventually, she made her way back to the roaring river, where she had found herself months ago. She stood by the bank and noticed several rocks with sharp edges on them at the water's edge. These will do, she thought to herself and carefully maneuvered herself down, so she could reach them without falling in. Taking a deep breath, she slammed her wing into the corner of a large grey rock. After three tries, she was no closer to getting rid of them. All there was to show of her failed attempts was a small trail of blood that trickled down her feathers.

At that very moment, she heard someone scream, "STOP THAT!!"

Rain looked up but didn't see anyone, so she just shook her head and went to hit the rock once more.

The voice shouted once again, "I SAID, STOP THAT!"

Realizing that she wasn't imagining the voice, she looked all around her, and, finally, made eye contact with the big grey elephant across the river.

"What the heck are you doing?" Ellie, the elephant, yelled over the rushing water.

Startled, Rain stood there and stared, not sure of how to respond.

"I asked you a question," the elephant continued, a bit softer. "Why are you trying to hurt yourself?"

"I'm not trying to hurt myself," Rain scoffed as if it was a ridiculous question.

"Sure looks like it from here."

"Well, looks can be deceiving," Rain responded; she noted the irony in her statement.

"Fair enough. Then tell me why it is that you're slamming yourself into a rock?"

Rain remained quiet for a moment, realizing how crazy she must have looked. Just hearing that question brought the reality of the situation to life. The longer she thought about it, the more embarrassed she became about her silly decision. What made it worse was that the elephant had seen and questioned her about it.

"Nothing," she answered after a momentary pause. "I wasn't doing anything. I ... I slipped is all."

The elephant shook her head sadly and said even more softly than before, "I don't believe you. I know what I saw, and I want to help."

"HELP? Yeah, right. Just leave me alone. I don't need anyone's help, especially not yours."

The young soul began to walk away as she had done before, but this time the elephant called out to her.

"You don't fool me, you know. You can act as tough as you'd like, but I've seen you around, mopey and sad, hidden away from everyone else. You have these incredible wings, and yet you never use them. Why is that?"

"Because I don't want to!" Rain challenged, fully expecting to hear how different and unworthy she was. She waited to be laughed and gawked at, and prepared herself for the elephant to just walk away like everyone else in her past had done.

But the elephant didn't move; she simply smiled and waited.

Finally, Rain's bitterness was overcome by the possibility of having someone to talk to after all those days and nights filled with silence. Rain let down her guard.

"The animals don't understand me; they won't accept me, and they don't want to be around me."

"Why is that?" the elephant asked nonchalantly.

"What do you mean? I'm a Pegasus, a horse, AND a bird; I don't fit in anywhere."

"I don't understand how that's a bad thing. As far as I can see, that just makes you special and lucky! Seems to me you would be the most popular animal in all the land!" Ellie exclaimed.

"HA!! It is the complete opposite of that," Rain said, and taking a deep breath, she told Ellie the whole story.

8

Rain started at the very beginning with the conversation she had with her teacher and the warnings given by the Creator. She recalled her encounters with the horses, birds, and the giraffe. She described what the monkeys had done to her; what she had ALLOWED them to do to her. She chose to live a lie to be a part of something, instead of being true to herself and eventually living alone. When all that backfired, the young soul decided that if forced to live a life in solitude, it would be her choice to do so, which is why the dense woods had become her forever home.

"Oh," Ellie said. After a few moments of thought, she continued. "I am not sure why that is your only choice."

"What other choices do I have?" Rain asked.

"When I look at you, I see a beautiful creature, full of love and curiosity. When I look into your eyes, I see hope and strength. When I look into your soul, I see so many beautiful colors. You are too smart to let the ignorance of others dictate your decisions or your happiness. When you met with the Creator, you were honest and true to who you are and who you felt you should be. Not everyone can identify who they really are, not to mention remaining true to it. That makes you very brave," Ellie said. "And to answer your question, there is another choice. You can come with me. My family will accept you as you are. We travel the world, and you can meet new creatures and see new places."

"I don't know," said Rain, unconvinced. "How do you know they won't be like all the rest and laugh at me?"

"Well, I'm not like all the rest, am I? I know you've had a tough time so far, but at some point, you will need to be with others and trust others. Why not start now?"

The young soul thought for a moment. "I suppose it couldn't hurt to try one last time. I can't possibly be any more unhappy than I am right now, so what harm could it really do? Okay, I'll give it a shot. But there's no way I can cross this river; it's way too big and fast. I'll never make it."

Ellie laughed. "Certainly not with those skinny little legs! I did notice you have a strong pair of wings that would definitely do the trick."

"Oh, no, no! I haven't used them in months. They're probably too weak," Rain sputtered.

The real reason she was against Ellie's plan was that she had been using her wings as an excuse for her unhappiness, acting as if they didn't exist. The thought of not only flying again but doing it in front of another animal terrified her. However, in this moment she couldn't deny that using her wings might forever change the course of her life, in a good way.

It had been so long that Rain wasn't even sure if her wings would work properly. She slowly allowed them to leave her sides. They were stiff, and her muscles began to ache, but it felt good to feel free to use them. After a few moments of stretching, she was able to get most of the kinks out. Ellie watched the leaves on the ground rustle as Rain's wings began to flap gently over the Earth. With a small smile upon her face, Rain backed up to get a running start and gracefully glided over the river, her hooves awkwardly slamming onto the Earth. To be on the side of the stream that had always been out of reach was a wonderful feeling.

Rain chuckled nervously. "I guess my landings could use a little work."

"Well, practice makes perfect," Ellie laughed back. "Now, let's get out of this sad, dark forest, and I'll show you to your new home." The elephant draped her trunk across the young soul's back and led them through the forest, over mountains, and through valleys until they came to a long flat plain. They stopped a few yards away from the largest watering hole Rain had ever seen. What was even more shocking to her were the dozens of animals in different shapes, sizes, colors, and species, all drinking and playing together, as if they were one.

Rain's mouth fell open in shock. "What is going on here? How is this possible?"

"This is my family," Ellie replied.

"Where? I don't see any other elephants?"

"Well, there are no other elephants here, but these creatures are all my family!"

"But everyone is so different."

"I told you, Rain. Here, we believe that what's inside is important, not what vessel you've been given or chosen. No one judges and no one discriminates."

"Wow. You're so lucky to have animals like that around you."

"Not me. Us," the gentle elephant reminded Rain.

"But, I'm not just another type of animal; I'm a whole new breed. It'll be a lot different for me than it is for all of you."

"Nonsense. You will be welcomed with open arms here, especially since you're 'different.'"

"But doesn't that just make us a group of 'misfits'? Doesn't that defeat the whole point of fighting for acceptance and staying away from being separated by breed?" Rain asked.

"If you look around, really look, you'll see that every animal is broken down into a combination of two or more creatures. Some who came first have had longer to expand their species than the rest. Everything is unique, from souls and animals to river rocks and snowflakes. A family is a group that cares about each other, protects, and loves each other. While we may seem like a group of 'misfits,' as you called them, that's what makes us special. We chose each other because of it, not despite it. Anyone is welcome to join us, but, unfortunately, many species still aren't ready to see beyond physical appearances. I genuinely believe that one day this will all change, and I think it's starting already," Ellie said confidently.

Seeing the doubtful expression on Rain's face, Ellie knew that words alone were not going to be enough to convince her. She thought for a second and then plucked one of the wiry hairs from her tail, twisted it into a circle, and offered it to Rain. "Here, take this."

"What it is?" the young soul asked, her head tilted in curiosity. "Wait! I recognize this. I've seen it before."

Ellie remained silent, allowing Rain to try and figure it out for herself.

"At the RIVER!" she finally exclaimed. "There was one by the river, next to a flower … wait … did you put that there? Did you leave it for me?"

"Perhaps," Ellie responded, her smile giving her away.

"I'm so sorry I just left it there. I didn't know what it was, and then I got distracted and—"

"It's okay!" Ellie interrupted. "You weren't ready for it then, but you are now."

"Well, what is it? What does it do?"

"Do? Nothing. It's just a circle. You see, I was once where you are now, sad and alone, and a stranger found me as I have found you and gave me a circle just like this; mine woven with fur. I still carry the circle with me to this day to remind me that I am loved." To validate her story, she pulled a yellow circle out from behind her ear. It was old and worn, fraying at the sides.

Rain studied the fur intensely. "But, you're so normal,"

she stated. "And elephants have been around forever. It couldn't have been hard for you to find a family. Why were you so sad and alone?"

Ellie chuckled. "Well, what does normal mean, really? Just because I look the same as my tribe physically doesn't mean I am the same inside. I didn't want to do what all the other elephants wanted to do. I wanted to be friends with all kinds of animals and go to places for reasons other than finding food and for survival. That's why I was cast out. Because I enjoyed and believed in things that they didn't understand. Not all differences are visible. The important thing to remember is the best part of being different is knowing that there will always be someone else who will share your feelings and appreciate you because of them. This circle that I was given has taught me that, and I hope yours will do the same for you."

Rain reluctantly took the circle and looked at Ellie. "Are you sure?"

"Absolutely," Ellie reassured.

"Thank you. Thank you so much for everything," said the young soul.

Rain took the circle and hooked it around her ear as Ellie had, keeping it close in case she needed reminding. Ellie just smiled and motioned towards the watering hole. With her newfound confidence, Rain spread her wings wide and beamed with pride she had never known possible. The young soul looked over at her new friend and smiled.

The two continued walking together, and when they reached the water's edge, they were greeted with smiles and immediate acceptance from all the other animals. Rain was elated and even received some compliments on her wings. It was then that she knew. Finally, this beautiful soul had found a family.

While this newfound acceptance thrilled her, the thought of all the others still out there living alone continued to upset her. She thought about Charlie a lot, saddened and confused by her betrayal, and she wondered what had become of her. Had she finally gotten what she wanted all along? Was it worth betraying and losing her friend? Rain shook her head and pushed the thoughts of Charlie out of her head. *What's done is done, no sense obsessing over it,* she told herself. Next, she thought of Zeek but was comforted knowing he had a family and wouldn't end up alone. She also thought of the narwhal and his sadness. Rain made up her mind at that moment to offer him a home with her new family. The least she could do was try and extend her good fortune to him.

A few days later, Rain, Ellie, and a few others who offered to take the trip up North—Gale, a tiger who had lost an eye in a fight; Jax, a crow whose feathers were an icy blue; and Stanley, a pig who looked "normal" from the outside but hated to be dirty, unlike most pigs—started on their journey.

Rain realized how lucky she was as they walked along

together, and just before she was going to share this with the group, she found herself face-to-face with the monkeys—the same monkeys who had tormented her so long ago. She stood there awkwardly, trying to decide what to do.

"What's happening?" Gale asked.

"Yeah, who are they? Do you know them? Why are we stopping?" Jax chimed in.

"Shhh," Ellie insisted, "Give her a minute."

"HORRID!!" the monkeys blurted. They started cackling and tossing moss in their direction.

"These are ... the monkeys. I never asked their names because all they ever did was taunt me and throw moss at me," Rain said, physically affected by their presence. "And I let them. I came every day and let them do it to me because I thought it was the only way I could belong." Rain stood there and let them bully her once again. It was as if no time had passed, and all the confidence she had gained disappeared in an instant. She tried focusing on the circle that Ellie had given her, but even that couldn't help her find her voice.

"STOP THAT! You stop that at ONCE!" Ellie shouted. The monkeys froze, surprised by her outburst. Not sure of how to respond, the monkeys just tilted their heads and waited for an explanation. Jax began flying around the monkeys, dive-bombing them and causing a commotion while Gale started pacing back and forth, baring her teeth in a threatening manner.

Ellie was instantly frustrated by her family's behavior and shouted at them too. "JAX and GALE! What are you two doing? Knock it off!"

"We're giving them a taste of their own medicine, of course!" Jax answered for both of them.

"Well, two wrongs don't make a right. Treating them as poorly as they treated Rain makes you just as bad as them!"

"Oh," said Gale. "Guess we didn't think of it like that." Gale stopped pacing, and Jax landed protectively on Rain's back.

Ellie turned back towards the monkeys. "What you did to Rain is wrong. You shouldn't treat others like that, ever. You should treat others as you would like to be treated, no matter how different they look or act," she finished, pointing her trunk at them as a mother does with her finger when she's scolding her young.

The monkeys said nothing, but they hung their heads, feeling bad for their actions. Out from the back of the group, a young monkey came running over to Rain, climbed up her feathers, and gave her a big hug around her neck. Rain froze, unsure of what was happening.

"I always liked you. You were brave. When I grow up, I'm going to be brave, just like you," whispered the monkey, and just as quickly as she had come, she was gone, following the humbled monkeys back into the trees.

All eyes were on Rain, but she did not know what to

say. Finally, she managed to get out a single word. "Brave?"

"Why do you say it like it's a question?" asked Stanley.

"I was not brave! I was a coward. I came back to them, day after day, for the sole purpose of getting bullied!"

"No. It was a means to an end. It's true, you should never let people hurt you like that, but you were doing what you thought you had to do to survive. Eventually, you got away from them and started treating yourself better. You never gave up. That is bravery," Stanley said matter-of-factly.

"I suppose that makes sense," Rain admitted. "Anyway, that's all behind me now. Let's keep moving. We still have a long way to go."

Jax remained settled on Rain's back as they continued on their way.

A few days had passed. Rain and her friends were laughing at Stanley, who had been telling them tall tales about his messy, messy family.

"And my SISTER!! She was the worst of the bunch! This one time she had these banana peels and ..." he trailed off as a group of horses came into view. "Are those the horses you used to live with?" he asked, his story quickly forgotten.

"Yes," Rain said emotionless, although her body quivered all over. She focused on her circle as she had done before, and this time found her inner strength. Rain gathered all the courage she could muster and flew over to them, showcasing her majestic wings. "Hello," she said, landing right in front of the Alpha.

"What are you doing here? Didn't we tell you to stay away?" the Alpha snarled, irritated by her brazen entrance.

Rain stood her ground, ignoring the question. Instead, she countered with, "Where is Charlie?" That was the real reason Rain was standing before them; she wanted the Alpha to know this.

"Charlie? That's why you came all the way back here?" the Alpha snorted. "Charlie is gone. We kicked her out right after we kicked YOU out!"

"What? Why would you kick her out? She told you my secret. She sold me out to get in your good graces."

"Is that what you've thought all those years? Charlie didn't give you up! We saw you flying around at night, and when we confronted her, she tried to deny it! Can you imagine? WE SAW YOU! If Charlie had just told us the truth, maybe we would have let her stay, but she took your side and tried to protect you. Neither of you are as smart as you think you are!" the Alpha finished, an evil laugh escaping her lips.

Ellie, who had been standing silently beside Rain, had finally reached her breaking point. "How dare you speak to her like that! Who do you think you are?" she barked, continuing to give them the same speech about acceptance and tolerance that she had given before, her angry tone cutting through the air.

The Alpha begrudgingly listened to what Ellie had to say, but it didn't seem to impact her the way it did the monkeys.

"We live how we choose to live and do what we want to do. If you don't like that, you are free to leave," she shot back, directing her next words to Rain. "Looks like you got what you wanted; a family of 'misfits,' just like you."

Disgusted with their ignorance, Ellie turned to the others. "Come on, let's get out of here, away from all this negativity." She trumpeted loudly, startling the horses, and began to walk away. Stanley turned and kicked up some dirt, Gale barred her teeth at the group more aggressively then she had with the monkeys, and Jax, once again, dive-bombed the group, which caused them to scatter.

As the five of them ventured off, they loudly threw out insults and made jokes on the horses' behalf. Even though Ellie was still full of rage, she knew she had to step up again as the voice of reason.

"I know and understand how upset you all are, and it's really sweet that you want to stand up for Rain and protect her, but calling the horses names is what they did to her. We've behaved badly enough already. We need to let it go and move forward."

"WHATTTT?" Gale exclaimed, "Just let it go?? After what she said to her? After what she said about us?"

"I know it's hard not letting it bother you, but we know better. What you have to understand is that not everyone knows better. Sometimes other animals are raised like that and are taught to feel like that. Others have had things happen in their lives that caused them to act up. Sometimes, it's not all their fault."

"Not their fault?" Jay chimed in. "Then whose fault is it?"

Ellie sighed, trying to figure out how to help them understand the point she was trying to make.

"All I'm saying is that sometimes good souls do bad things without even realizing it. It is not an excuse, of course, but if we have hatred towards them in our hearts without understanding the full situation, we are just as guilty as they are."

"I guess I can see what you're saying, but I can't see how the Alpha doesn't realize that the way she treats others who are different is wrong," Jax huffed.

"I know," Ellie said. "Perhaps it's because no one stands up to her, and her family just lets her behave this way. Maybe she feels like she has to act like that to protect herself and her tribe, or maybe it's just her pride. I don't really have the answer, but I do know that we are better than that and shouldn't let her thoughtless words upset us."

"Fine," Jax conceded. "But I still don't like her."

"Fair enough," Ellie chuckled, breaking up the tension. "Truth be told, I don't particularly care for her either."

Stanley, Jax, and Gale joined in on the laughter and picked up their pace, ready to leave the whole situation behind them. Rain had only been half-listening to the conversation because all she could think about was what the Alpha had said about Charlie. *She hadn't given up on me, she had tried to keep my secret, and she got punished for it. Now, she's out there alone, and it's all my fault. Why didn't I just give her a chance to speak? I bullied her!* Guilt ran through her; she knew that she would need to find Charlie before she returned home. Find her, beg for forgiveness, and invite her to come live with her and be part of her family.

"Rain! HELLO!" Jax squawked, trying to get her attention.

"Yes, what?" she answered, snapping back to reality.

"Let's goooo! What are you doing?"

"I'm coming, I'm coming," she said and caught up to the rest of the group, not quite ready to tell them about her future plan.

9

It took two weeks to trek to the icy waters where the Narwhal lived. But finally, they arrived at the bank of the ocean.

"MR. NARWHAL!" Rain yelled over the sea. "HELLO? ARE YOU HERE?"

But all that answered back was silence.

"Maybe he moved away?" Stanley offered.

"Maybe," Rain said sadly, worried that the narwhal had gone back up to the universe early and endangered his soul.

Just then, the water began to ripple, and a baby narwhal emerged.

"Oh," said Rain, startled. "Hi there, little one."

The baby looked at her as he slowly bobbed up and

down in the water. Moments later, the sea shifted again, and out popped two more narwhals. Rain recognized one of them immediately. The narwhal, however, wasn't so sure.

"You look so familiar. How do I know you? Wait, I know! You're the Pegasus who came to see me a while back," he said confidently. "Am I remembering that correctly? What are you doing here?"

"YES! We met at this same spot years ago. I've come to see you!" she answered and motioned towards the other narwhals. "Is this your family?"

"Yes, it is! This is my wife, Nancy, and our son, Noah," he said proudly, and as he turned toward the group, he was struck with the realization that he was unable to proceed with the introductions. "I'm sorry, Pegasus, I can't recall your name."

"My name is Rain. If I remember correctly, you never got around to telling me yours," Rain said slyly.

"Ah, yes. Well, I wasn't in the best place back then. My sincere apologies for that. My name is Ned."

"Well, hi, Ned! Nice to meet you … again," Rain said, laughing, and the whole group chimed in. "This is Stanley, Ellie, Jax, and Gale! They're MY family!"

"Pleasure is all mine! So, tell me, Rain, why did you come to see me after all this time?"

"I just wanted to make sure you were okay. You were as sad and lonely as I was back then, and though it took a while, I eventually found a family. Well, they found me," she said, smiling at Ellie. I've thought about you a lot over the years and wondered if you had been lucky enough to have found one also. If you hadn't, I was going to invite you to be a part of our family, but it looks like you have done quite well on your own, and I'm glad to see you so happy!'

"Thank you," he said. "I appreciate your kind words and that generous offer."

"Wow," exclaimed Nancy, "how thoughtful of you! You must have really made an impression on her, honey," she said to Ned.

"I was a total jerk to Rain," he said sheepishly. "I have no idea how you even remembered me, never mind wanting to come back here to see me! I'm truly sorry that that was our only interaction. I really am a nice guy."

"Humph," Nancy snorted. "Sounds like you weren't very nice to her!"

Ned sighed. "In those days, I didn't know how I would go on living. I was so sad and lonely and couldn't see what was right in front of me. I know there is no excuse for my behavior, and I hope you can forgive me."

"Aw, no," Rain insisted, "You were fine."

"No, I wasn't. I just left you to fend for yourself in a place and climate you were unfamiliar with, especially during the peak of the season! And I should have recognized that you were just as disheartened as I was, and accepted your offer of friendship."

"Ned, it's okay. You were having a hard time. We both were. My memory of that day is completely different than yours. I admired your resolve to stick it out and make decisions based on your mind and not your heart. That helped me to survive alone for a very long time. Besides, I'm pretty sure our conversation got interrupted by a storm, so ..." Rain grinned.

"Yeah, righttttt. It was all because of the storm," Ned said, laughing at her joke.

"You know, you and your family are always welcome to come back with us," Ellie offered.

"Thank you so much," Ned responded, "but we have built ourselves a happy home here. And I don't think we could really thrive in the warmer waters that you are accustomed to."

"You're probably right about that," Stanley agreed. "However, you don't have to come back with us to be a part of our family. Families live apart all the time, but it doesn't mean they're not still in our hearts."

"That's absolutely right!" Nancy joined in. "Oh, and everyone will think we're so cool when we tell them we have family down South, who live on LAND!"

Everyone shared a laugh.

"I guess it's settled then!" Rain said joyously. "Family."

Stanley, checking the sky as always, noticed some dark storm clouds in the distance. "I hate to break this up, but it looks like there's another nasty storm coming."

They all looked up, and Rain smirked. "See, darn storm coming and ruining everything … again!"

Ned smiled. "You should probably get going. These storms can get quite destructive. It was so great to see you again and meet your family. And please, don't be strangers!"

"Oh, we'll be back," Rain promised, and the others nodded behind her.

After they said their goodbyes, the five friends began their long journey back home. After her recent run-in with the horses, Rain grew discouraged. But now, she was filled with a new sense of hope. Rain had assumed that after all of the time that had passed, the horses would have softened a bit, making them more accepting, but clearly, they hadn't. But then she thought about how the monkeys had reacted and how Ned apologized for things she hadn't even noticed. Perhaps Ellie's words about being patient and allowing time for things to change were true. Maybe one day, it would also include the horses. She had found a family, and now Ned had as well, paving the way for more and more species to thrive. Maybe souls that made decisions as she had, ones who couldn't identify with a more conventional form, would have an easier time then she had. Perhaps soon, all of Earth's creatures would stop being so judgmental and just accept everyone's unique characteristics.

10

WHILE A MASSIVE WEIGHT HAD been lifted off her shoulders, Rain couldn't shake her guilt over what had happened with Charlie. She had hoped to run into her at some point during the journey, but they were now only a few days out, and she realized it wasn't going to happen. The trek had been a long one, and they had all grown tired; their usual chatty banter replaced by silence, save for a few grunts here and there.

Rain stopped abruptly, her decision made. "You all go on ahead of me. I have something I need to take care of."

"Whatttttt??" Jax shrieked.

Stanley rolled his eyes at Jax's overly dramatic response, then turned towards Rain.

"What is it you need to do?"

"I need to find Charlie and make amends, make sure she's okay, and beg forgiveness."

Gale grunted disapprovingly. "But she gave you up!"

"That's not what the Alpha said. She said she didn't give me up, and that's why they kicked her out."

"And you believe her? With all of her obvious bad habits, I'm sure lying is in her arsenal as well."

"I do. The Alpha is many things, but one thing she never misses is an opportunity to recall a story in which she taught someone a lesson. I made an assumption, and I was wrong, and now she's out there all alone."

"You don't know that she's all alone," Stanley offered.

"You're right. I don't know. But assuming that she found a family just isn't good enough. I've already made that mistake. I need to know for sure, either way."

"All right, enough talking about it. Let's start looking," suggested an exhausted Ellie.

"What? No, Ellie; while I appreciate the offer, I know how exhausted all of you are. You have done so much for me already. Please, finish your journey home," Rain insisted. "This is probably something I should do on my own, anyway."

The others stood there, looking at Ellie, not sure what to do.

"What are you waiting for? She told you to go home, so on with it!" Jax chirped.

Rain looked at him. "I said all of you. Jax, that includes you."

"I'm not going back with them. Don't be silly. You're not just wandering around out here all alone, and besides, I have wings too. It will be much easier to find her with both of us looking, so we'll be able to cover twice as much ground."

While Rain wanted to argue this point, she knew Jax was right.

"Okay, fine. Thanks, Jax."

"Excellent! Let's go!" he said, already darting into the sky.

"Well, then," Rain laughed, "I guess I'll be saying goodbye for both of us. Thank you all again for everything. I wish you a quick and uneventful journey home."

Stanley tilted his head. "Stop making it out like you're never going to see us again. Go and find Charlie and come back home. We'll see you there soon."

"Okay, okay. See you soon!" Rain said right before she too took to the sky, trying to catch up to Jax.

The two flew over mountains and valleys, above forests and lakes with no trace of Charlie.

"Where can she be?" Rain asked out loud.

"Are there any special places she likes to hang out? Any secret hideaways?" Jax offered.

Rain thought for a minute about secret hideaways. "OF COURSE!" she yelled. Without another word, Rain took off at full speed, leaving a confused Jax in her wake.

After an hour or so of flying, Rain landed on the outskirts of a small wooded area. Jax, who had struggled to keep up with her, plopped down on the ground, exhausted.

"Where are we?" he mumbled.

"There is a hidden pond in there that we used to go to so that I could swim freely without the other horses finding out about my secret. I just hope that she still comes here."

Once the two ventured through the woods and came upon the pond, Rain saw that her search was finally over. There stood Charlie, sipping the crystal water, and Rain couldn't help but shriek with joy.

Startled by the sound, Charlie jumped and spun around.

"Rain?" she exclaimed, "Is that really you?"

"Yes, it's me! Is that really you?" Rain said in excitement, and without thinking, ran over to Charlie and gave her a nuzzle. But Charlie pulled away.

"Wait! You're not mad at me anymore?" she asked hesitantly.

"Mad at YOU? No, no, of course, not! I have seen the Alpha, and she told me all about what happened after I was cast out. If anyone should be mad, it should be you. I should have let you talk, given you a chance to explain. I should never have assumed that you would sell me out." Rain said, apologizing wholeheartedly.

"There's no need for that. The whole situation was terrible. If I were you, I probably would have reacted the same way. The Alpha is good at that, making you feel like at the end of the day, you're all alone and can't trust anyone, no matter what the situation is."

"Perhaps that's true," Rain countered, "but I can't help feeling bad. Have you been alone this whole time?"

"Yeah, but it was fine. I don't mind being alone, and after all that stuff happened, well, it was a much better option than cowering to them, especially since you were the best part of being back. Once you were gone, there was really no point in trying to fight my way back in. But that's enough about me," Charlie said, trying to change the subject. "Why did you come to find me? And who is that little blue crow hiding behind you?"

"Oh, how rude of me. This is Jax. He came to help me find you."

"Well, hello there, Jax. Nice to meet you," Charlie offered.

"Hello," Jax replied sheepishly.

"Jax! Since when are you so shy?" Rain declared.

"I'm not shy," Jax replied, puffing his chest up. "I just wanted to give you two time to talk, and well ... I've never seen such a small horse before."

"I'm a pony, actually," Charlie informed him before she turned back to Rain. "So, I guess you finally found a family, and with the birds! I'd never have guessed that, but it makes sense."

Rain smiled. "Actually, my family is made up of all sorts of animals. There's an elephant, a tiger, a pig, and so many more!"

"That's incredible," Charlie said with amazement. "I'm so happy you finally found a family. You had wanted one so badly."

"I did, and I am so grateful to them. They've supported me in ways I never knew I needed," she said wistfully. "Speaking of family, we should really get back home. We've been gone for so long, and I miss them dearly."

"Oh, yeah, okay. I get it. Well, it was so nice to see you, and I'm really glad we were able to clear the air. Despite what happened, I have always considered you my sister."

"Nice to see me? What are you talking about? You're

coming with us, of course!" Jax squawked. "You really think we'd come all the way out here just to say hi?"

Charlie just stared at them, stunned.

Rain laughed. "While that wasn't at all how I would have put it, he's right. We did come here to find you and bring you back with us."

"You mean it? You really want me to? You think it would be okay?"

"What do you mean, 'okay'?"

"Well, you know. I'm a pony. Even Jax said he's never even seen a pony before and—"

"Charlie, weren't you listening to me? It doesn't matter that you're different. Where we're going, it's considered a GOOD thing. Now, come on, let's get a move on. We have at least a week of traveling ahead of us."

While Charlie's eyes danced with excitement, her heart was still hesitant. Like Rain, she had lived through her share of disappointment and rejection, and it was not easy for her to trust anyone, even her long-lost sister. Rain noticed this and was struck with an idea. She reached up and took the thin black circle from her ear, handed it to Charlie, and repeated Ellie's words.

"No one has ever given me anything before," Charlie said, full of emotion, studying the circle that was passed from Ellie to Rain. "It's beautiful."

After that, Charlie placed the circle over her ear and agreed to go with them. As the three slowly made their way back to the plains, Rain and Jax filled Charlie in on all of their adventures. When they finally arrived at the watering hole, they were greeted with cheers and nuzzles. Finally, they were ALL home.

Ellie noticed the circle around Charlie's ear and smiled.

Epilogue

Ellie, Rain, Charlie, and the others spent many years together, traveling the world, forging new and unique friendships, making memories, and, most importantly, learning from each other.

Everyone has a different journey and a different story. Don't forget to put yourself in someone else's shoes before you pass judgment! Always hear people out. Ask for forgiveness when you're wrong and offer forgiveness to others who are genuinely sorry.

As for the circle, it has been passed on year after year, century after century. It has become a symbol of love and a reminder that sometimes even the things you don't like about yourself, the ones that make you "different" are the ones that others love the most. Always be true to yourself, and remember that being different is a good thing because that's what makes you special.

Acknowledgments

Em, thank you for being so dedicated, patient, and nonjudgmental throughout this whole process. You had more faith in me than I had in myself, and without you, this book never would have come to fruition.

Mom and Dad, thank you for all your help, support, and love.

Bella, Tori, and Jules, thank you for all your input and advice.

About the Author

Born and raised in Brewster, New York, Sara Larca discovered her passion for writing while doing the things she loves most: taking photographs and traveling the world. Her first book, *Hidden Wings*, is inspired by events in the lives of close friends, as well as personal experience. It was her desire to spread a message of hope and understanding, coupled with her special connection to elephants, that helped this story and its characters come to life. In her free time she enjoys baking, drawing, reading, and spending time with her friends and family.